Ripplestripe and the Peace Locket

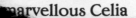

marvellous Celia

Special thanks to Valerie Wilding

ORCHARD BOOKS

First published in Great Britain in 2021 by The Watts Publishing Group

1 3 5 7 9 10 8 6 4 2

Text copyright © 2021 Working Partners Limited
Illustrations © Orchard Books 2021
Series created by Working Partners Limited

A CIP catalogue record for this book is available from the British Library.

ISBN 978 1 40836 392 8

Printed and bound in Great Britain by Clays Ltd, Elcograf S.p.A.

The paper and board used in this book are made from wood from responsible sources.

Orchard Books
An imprint of Hachette Children's Group
Part of The Watts Publishing Group Limited
Carmelite House
50 Victoria Embankment
London EC4Y 0DZ

An Hachette UK Company

www.hachette.co.uk
www.hachettechildrens.co.uk

Contents

Aisha and Emily are best friends from Spellford Village. Aisha loves sports, whilst Emily's favourite thing is science. But what both girls enjoy more than anything is visiting Enchanted Valley and helping their unicorn friends, who live there.

Rosymane

Rosymane is the first of the Healing Crystal Unicorns, whose magical lockets help to keep all the creatures of Enchanted Valley feeling well.

Firebright's special
healing magic looks after
the inside of the body –
everything from a cold
to a tummy ache.

Firebright

Twinkleshade

Twinkleshade's healing
crystal has the power to
soothe worries away
and help everyone
feel calm.

Ripplestripe uses
her amazing magic
to heal the heart.
She helps to mend
friendships after
arguments.

Ripplestripe

Spellford

Enchanted Valley

Enchanted Cottage

Golden Palace

An Enchanted Valley lies a twinkle away,
Where beautiful unicorns live, laugh and play.
You can visit the mermaids, or go for a ride,
So much fun to be had, but dangers can hide!

Your friends need your help – this is how you know:
A keyring lights up with a magical glow.
Whirled off like a dream, you won't want to leave.
Friendship forever, when you truly believe.

Chapter One
A Mean Girl

Emily Turner knelt in the sand and picked up her yellow spade. "*Oh, I do like to be beside the seaside*," she sang.

"Me, too," said her best friend, Aisha Khan, as she turned her bucket upside down.

The girls and their parents had all come

to spend a day by the sea. They had hired a beach hut, and Mr Khan was busy preparing a delicious picnic. People all around were having fun paddling, playing games or whizzing frisbees to each other.

Emily and Aisha were building an enormous sand palace.

Mrs Turner strolled down to take a look. "That's amazing!" she said.

"Thanks, Mum!" said Emily. "We're going to make it even better. Just wait and see!"

"It looks magical," her mum said. "What imagination you girls have!"

Aisha and Emily shared a smile. They couldn't tell Mrs Turner they were building a copy of a real palace – Queen Aurora's palace!

Aisha and Emily shared a wonderful secret. There was a beautiful place called Enchanted Valley which they often visited, using magic! The girls had enjoyed so many adventures there. They'd made friends with dragons, elves, mermaids and lots of other fantastic creatures. But their very special friends were the unicorns, including Queen Aurora, who ruled over Enchanted Valley.

"I'll let you know when the food's ready," Emily's mum said. She bent to rub sun lotion into each of their noses, and

then went back to the beach hut.

The girls upended their buckets to create two towers. "Let's do the turrets," said Aisha. These were tricky. Aurora's palace had golden turrets that twisted like unicorn horns! They shaped the damp sand with their hands.

When they were finished, Emily and Aisha sat back and looked proudly at the sand palace.

Just then, a girl with pretty dark curls ran over. Emily looked up and smiled.

"Hello," said Aisha.

The girl didn't reply. Instead, she glared at their sand sculpture. She took a step back, and another — then she took a running jump straight into the middle of the sand palace. The towers and turrets collapsed. Then she laughed.

The girls stared in shock.

Emily leaped to her feet. "What did you do that for?" she cried.

"We worked really hard on that!" said Aisha. She felt so cross and upset.

The girl laughed again. "Who cares?"

she said. "It was a rubbish sandcastle." The girl flicked sprays of sand over the ruins with her toes. Then she strolled away, laughing.

Aisha stared after her, open-mouthed. "You're mean and nasty!" she shouted.

Emily was so tearful she couldn't speak. She fished in her shorts pocket for a tissue, but her eye was caught by a soft glow coming from inside.

"Aisha, look!" she said.

The crystal unicorn keyring in her pocket was glowing!

Aisha quickly checked her own jumpsuit pocket. Her keyring was glowing too!

The keyrings were gifts from Queen Aurora. When they glowed, the girls knew she was calling them back to Enchanted Valley.

Aisha's eyes shone. "This means a new adventure!" she cried, but Emily raised a finger to her lips. The mean girl was still nearby, laughing at them. It wouldn't do to let her hear about their secret!

"Come on, Aisha," Emily said loudly, so the girl could hear. "Let's get an ice cream."

"Great idea," said Aisha. They told their parents where they were going then walked over to the ice cream van.

Instead of joining the queue, the girls ducked out of sight behind the van. They were off to Enchanted Valley! No time passed in the real world while they were there, so no one would know they were gone.

When Emily held her keyring out towards Aisha's, it felt as if powerful magnets were pulling them together. The unicorns' horns touched, and brilliantly coloured sparkles seemed to explode into the air. The sparkles whirled and

swirled, and the beach disappeared from view. Then the girls felt their feet lift off the ground. They clutched each other in excitement.

When their feet touched down once more, it wasn't on soft sand but on springy grass. The sparkles faded. Emily and Aisha tucked their keyrings into their pockets and looked around. They were standing at the bottom of the hill that led up to Queen Aurora's glittering golden palace. Pink and yellow flowers rambled over the walls, and the flags on the tall, twisting turrets fluttered in the warm breeze.

"We're back in Enchanted Valley!" Emily said happily.

Just then, the palace's silver drawbridge

lowered, and two unicorns appeared. In the lead was Queen Aurora. Her coat was like a summer sunrise, with shifting shades of red, orange, pink and yellow. She wore a small silver crown and her mane and tail gleamed gold in the bright sunshine.

A dazzling white unicorn with a silver mane and tail followed her. He wore a

circlet of crystals on his head that sparked
rainbow colours in the sunlight. He was
the kind and handsome Crystal King,
who was visiting from his kingdom,
Crystal Valley.

Queen Aurora came up to the girls and
pressed her velvety cheek against theirs.
"I'm so happy you're here," she said in
her gentle voice. "We're
desperate to get
Ripplestripe's
locket back."

Ripplestripe
was one of the
four Healing
Crystal Unicorns.
They wore magical

crystal lockets, which helped to keep everyone in Enchanted Valley healthy and happy. But a wicked unicorn called Selena had stolen all four lockets! She had refused to give them back unless Aurora handed over her crown and made Selena queen of Enchanted Valley. The girls knew they couldn't let that happen! Emily and Aisha had managed to get Firebright's and Rosymane's lockets back, so coughs and colds were cured again, and bumps and bruises were healed. They'd also saved Twinkleshade's locket, which healed worry and anxiety. But Selena still had Ripplestripe's Heart locket, which healed heartache, like pain after an argument or the ache in your

chest when a best friend went home after
a sleepover.

"The Crystal Festival is supposed to
start tonight," the king said anxiously.
"If we don't have all the Healing Crystal
lockets back by then, their magic will be
lost for ever."

Aurora looked so distressed that the girls
threw their arms around her neck.

"We can't let that happen!" cried Aisha.

"We won't," said Emily. "It would be a
disaster!"

"I knew you'd help us," said Queen
Aurora gratefully. "We must hurry.
Ripplestripe is waiting for us at the
Friendship Circle."

The girls glanced at one another.

They'd never heard of the Friendship
Circle before!

"It's where the Crystal Festival is held,"
explained the king. "We'll take you there.
Climb up!"

Aisha clambered up and buried her
hands in his silver mane, while Emily
climbed on to Aurora's back and clutched
her beautiful golden mane. Then the two

unicorns launched themselves into the clear blue sky of Enchanted Valley.

Emily and Aisha were determined to get Ripplestripe's locket back. But they knew that Selena would be just as determined to stop them.

Chapter Two
Flight to the Friendship Circle

They soared over Enchanted Valley's grassy meadows and forests, with the silvery river glinting below. Normally, there was nothing more wonderful than flying over a magical land on a unicorn's back, but right now the girls were too worried to feel the usual thrill.

As they flew beneath fluffy white clouds, Aisha saw a circle of huge stones set in a grassy dell. Each one stood twice as tall as a unicorn! They reminded her of a school trip to Stonehenge … until sunlight hit them.

The stones glittered and sparkled, sending out flashing darts of red, blue, green and gold. The girls gasped. They weren't stones after all, but tall crystals!

A river flowed gently beyond the circle, sparkling almost as brightly as the crystals. All around the valley, busy creatures were setting up for the festival. Brightly coloured lanterns hung in the trees, and the girls heard wind chimes tinkle as though they were singing.

As they landed, the girls spotted the beautiful striped blue coat of Ripplestripe, the Heart Healing Unicorn. She trotted over to greet them with a warm whinny. Different shades of blue – blueberry, ice blue and sky blue – mingled together

in her mane and tail. Behind her were
Firebright, Rosymane and Twinkleshade,
each with a gleaming locket around their
neck.

"Girls! You came!" Ripplestripe cried as
Emily and Aisha slipped off Aurora and
the Crystal King's backs.

Aisha stroked Ripplestripe's soft blue neck. "Don't worry, we'll help find your locket," she said.

"We've beaten Selena before, and we'll do it again," Emily promised.

The king said in a serious voice, "I hope you're right. The ceremony isn't just for charging the Healing Crystal lockets. It's when *all* the crystals in Enchanted Valley get charged with magic – including your keyrings." He moved closer and spoke quietly. "If they don't get charged tonight, you girls won't be able to travel between here and your own world ever again."

Emily and Aisha's insides churned.

"What if we get stuck here?" Emily asked in dismay.

Queen Aurora whinnied softly.

Aisha's eyes filled with tears. "We love our unicorn friends so much," she said, "but we couldn't bear never seeing our families and our own world again."

Emily hugged her. "Selena won't win," she said. "There's still time."

Just then, they heard an angry shout. They turned to see their friend Ember the phoenix arguing with another friend, Lumi the lightingale. "You dropped my banner, and now it's dirty! Say sorry!" said Ember.

"You dropped it, and you trod on it," Lumi said crossly. "*You* say sorry."

"Shan't!" said the phoenix.

"Ember! Lumi! What's wrong?" asked

Aisha.
"You're
usually
such good
friends."

Both birds
turned their
backs on
each other.

"Oh dear, they won't make up," said
Ripplestripe. "This is why we need my
locket."

The sky suddenly turned dark and
stormy. A flash of lightning made
everyone jump, and in the next moment
there was a rolling crash of thunder.
There was a chorus of squeals, squawks

and squeaks as frightened creatures scattered into the trees.

A silver unicorn swooped out of a grey cloud to land in front of the group. Her dark blue tail swished angrily, and sparks spat from her pointy horn.

"It's Selena!" cried Aisha.

The evil unicorn glared. "You horrible girls! Interfering again?" she snarled. "Well, you're not getting the last locket unless I get Aurora's crown. Time's running out, so if you want the crystal magic to work again, you'd better make me queen!"

Aurora took a cautious step towards Selena. "You will never be queen," she said quietly.

Emily noticed how Aurora's voice shook, and went to stand beside her. "Selena, we'll find that locket, you'll see!"

"Good luck with that," Selena sneered. She looked past the little group, and her ears flattened against her head.

"Why does she look nervous? What's she seen?" Emily murmured. She turned to see a brown otter climbing on to the riverbank.

"It's Slick!" she cried. "He's got the Heart locket around his neck."

"Grab him!" cried Aisha, diving for the otter.

But Selena screamed, "Get away, Slick! Now! Go far, far away! Hide that locket!"

Slick slithered away from Aisha and darted along the riverbank.

"Hide it well," Selena screeched after him. "If you let me down, there will be no sparkly things for you! GO!"

"After him!" cried Emily. She and Aisha raced along the bank.

Crash!

Flash!

A lightning bolt struck the ground in front of them. Aisha and Emily were thrown backwards. They landed with a great bump, surrounded by smoke from a burning patch of grass. Their legs trembled and their hearts pounded.

How could they possibly defeat such a nasty, spiteful unicorn?

Chapter Three
Magical Mermaid Combs

Two brave gnomes rushed to stamp out
the sparks that littered the grass, while
Aisha and Emily scrambled to their feet.

The Healing Crystal Unicorns came
running.

"Are you OK?" called Firebright, her
orange mane and tail streaming as she

cantered up. "Any bumps? Bruises?"

The girls shook their heads as they brushed themselves down.

"We're fine, thank you, Firebright," said Aisha.

"No bumps or bruises – but no otter, either," Emily added. "We've no idea where Slick's gone now."

"Oh yes we do," Aisha cried suddenly. She pointed to the mud of the riverbank. "Look! Paw prints!"

A trail of paw prints ran alongside the river for as far as they could see.

"Brilliant!" said Emily in delight. "We can track Slick and take that locket before he hides it."

"I'll come with you," said Ripplestripe.

"We'll stay here to guard the Friendship Circle," said Twinkleshade. Firebright and Rosymane nodded.

"And I must go back to the palace," said Queen Aurora. "Now that Selena's around again, I can't leave it unguarded. She could break in and take over!"

The Crystal King nodded. "You're right, Aurora," he said. "I'll go with you. I could never leave you to face Selena alone."

The queen touched her cheek to his. "Thank you," she said softly.

The royal unicorns wished their friends good luck, then flew off. The other Healing Crystal Unicorns trotted back to the gleaming crystal circle.

"Right. Time for us to get going, too,"

Emily said. She began to follow the muddy paw prints along the riverbank. Aisha followed Emily, and Ripplestripe cantered ahead. Soon, they'd left the Friendship Circle far behind. It was hard going, for the mud made them slip and slide.

After a while, Aisha climbed on to a

rock and shaded her eyes. Beyond a stretch of woodland, she saw the gleam of shining water.

"The lagoon!" she cried. "Maybe our mermaid friends have seen Slick."

The paw prints led right up to the edge of the lagoon, where they disappeared.

"He's gone into the water," Ripplestripe

said in disappointment. "How can we follow him now?"

Aisha grinned. "I know how," she said, "and I know just what we need."

Emily nodded, and they spoke together. "Magic combs!"

Ripplestripe looked puzzled until Aisha explained that the mermaids had let them borrow some combs on other adventures. "When we put them in our hair, they magically transform us into mermaids."

"Wow!" said Ripplestripe, swishing her blue tail in excitement. "Do you think I could transform too?"

"No harm in trying!" said Aisha.

"We'll look for our mermaid friend, Pearl," said Emily.

They ran along the edge of the lagoon, until they found Pearl lazing in a rock pool. Her hair hung around her shoulders and her little mermaid tail flipped against a stone. She was weaving a seaweed bracelet, and looked a little grumpy.

"Aisha! Emily!" she said. "I'm happy to see you!"

"You don't *look* very happy, Pearl," said Emily.

"Oh, it's nothing," said the mermaid. "I had an argument with my sister, Opal, and I'm still annoyed with her."

The girls glanced at each other. This had to be the missing locket's effect. Pearl and Opal hardly ever quarrelled!

Aisha introduced Pearl to Ripplestripe, and explained why they needed the combs.

To their delight, Pearl had seen Slick. "I know where he's gone," she said. "Down into the water! Wait here. I'll fetch some combs."

She disappeared into the lagoon, and was back a few moments later with three shiny white combs. Each held a sparkling blue sea sapphire.

Aisha and Emily kicked off their sandals and slipped into the water, followed by

Ripplestripe, who placed her hooves carefully between the rocks until the water lapped up to her tummy.

When the girls put the combs in their hair, and Pearl put one in Ripplestripe's mane, the water around them began to move, gently at first. Then it swirled faster, and faster still. The girls felt their legs tingle as their feet lifted off the sandy bottom.

Then they looked down to see tails appear where their legs had been a moment ago, and their crystal keyrings hung from little belts of plaited seaweed.

Ripplestripe gasped. "I have a mermaid tail!" she cried and swished it, spinning around and around as the scales glittered like little rainbow crescents in the sunshine. "I look like a kelpie!"

The girls had met kelpies before on their adventures. They were magical water

creatures with horses' heads and front legs, and mermaids' tails.

Aisha grinned. "You'll be able to talk and breathe underwater like a kelpie, too!"

Emily slapped the water with her tail. "OK, everyone," she said. "Let's find that otter!"

Chapter Four
Cousin Neptune

"I saw Slick disappear into the Corkscrew Current," said Pearl. "This way." She dived underwater and the friends followed her.

"I've read about currents in my *Big Book of Science*," said Emily, as they swam. "They're streams of water that move very fast inside seas and rivers."

"Exactly," said Pearl.

They followed the mermaid out of the warm lagoon and into the sea, until they saw something that looked like a swirling, curling water slide. But it had no sides to hold on to – it was just water!

"This is it," said Pearl, "our Corkscrew Current."

It looked like water rushing down a giant plughole, but it swirled much faster.

Emily moved closer. "Hey, it looks like *two* corkscrews, twisting around each other!"

"You're right," said Pearl. "The water in one corkscrew leads down all the way to Glimmer City, and the other one leads back here."

Aisha and Emily felt a rush of excitement.

"Glimmer City?" said Emily. "That sounds amazing!"

"It is," said Pearl. "It's a magical underwater city, where my cousin Neptune lives. And I'm pretty sure I saw the otter dive into the current that would take him there. Maybe he's planning to hide your locket in the city, Ripplestripe."

The friends couldn't wait to get going, but Pearl held up a hand. "I'll send Neptune a message first, asking him to help you when you arrive." She led them back to the surface. Then she cupped her hands around her mouth and gave a strange warbling call. Aisha thought it

sounded like water running over pebbles
in a stream.

A long, slender creature flew across the
lagoon towards Pearl. It was a fish! His
large fins were shaped like aeroplane
wings.

"A flying
fish!" Aisha
cried in
delight.

"This is
my friend,
Airy," said Pearl.
"Airy, will you take a message to
Neptune, please? Tell him I'm sending
Aisha, Emily and Ripplestripe to
Glimmer City. They need his help." Her

face grew serious. "It's very important."

"Message received," said Airy. "On my way." He flapped his fins once and launched himself up, up, high into the air. Then he turned, folding the fins flat against his body. Down he dived, down, down towards the lagoon, gathering speed until he disappeared beneath the surface with scarcely a splash.

"Airy's the fastest messenger in the sea," said Pearl. "Now, simply dive headfirst into the Corkscrew Current. Don't worry – you'll love the ride!"

Aisha thanked her. She was a little bit nervous, but trusted Pearl. She gathered herself and – one, two, three! – plunged in. Behind her, she sensed Emily and

Ripplestripe following. The water was so warm! It whisked them along, down and around, around and down.

"Whee!" cried Emily. "This is so much fun!"

Aisha squealed in delight. "It's like a twisty helter-skelter!" She glanced back to see Ripplestripe's excited face and her blue mane streaming behind her.

They passed shoals of colourful fish, mermaids playing tag with dolphins, and once they rushed past two teams of white kelpies playing tideball. But the ball bobbed about by itself while the kelpies argued.

"Oh no!" Ripplestripe called. "If I had my locket, they would soon make up.

I've never known so many quarrels in Enchanted Valley."

The current carried the friends deeper and deeper until it slowed and finally spilled them out. They tumbled through a sign shaped like a hoop. Sparkly letters spelled out "Welcome to Glimmer City"!

The three friends drifted to the sandy

floor of the lagoon. Nearby was an entrance to a tunnel made of coral in all sorts of different hues – emerald, pink and bright orange.

A merman was waiting for them. His hair was the colour of red–brown seaweed and his tanned face broke into a huge smile as he greeted the visitors.

"I'm Neptune," he said and took each of the girls by the hand. "You must be Aisha and Emily."

"Hello," said Emily.

"Thanks for meeting us," added Aisha.

Neptune turned to the unicorn. "And you're Ripplestripe. I'm proud to help you. Airy told me you're looking for a very naughty otter," he added. "Well, he's arrived, and he's already quite annoying."

Emily, Aisha and Ripplestripe followed Neptune through the tunnel. Neptune's red-brown hair gleamed in the light shining from up ahead.

Suddenly they were out of the tunnel and in the centre of a big, beautiful square. "Welcome to Glimmer City," Neptune said proudly. "This is Seagrass Square."

Pretty coral cottages adorned with shells clustered around the square. They shimmered with a gentle light. In the middle of the square was a fountain standing in a great bowl made of shining mother-of-pearl.

Emily and Aisha both gasped so hard, big bubbles burst out of their mouths.

"Wow!"

"Look!" Emily cried. "It's not a water fountain, it's a sand fountain!"

Sand of ever-changing colours arced out of the fountain, drifting back down into the pearly bowl.

All sorts of creatures swam through the square. There were mermaids with merbabies, seahorses out shopping, a smiling purple octopus and even a friendly kelpie who said hello to Ripplestripe.

"It's magical!" said Aisha.

They swam past an umbrella-shaped creature with long multicoloured tentacles. He giggled as he told a joke to his friends, who fell about laughing.

"They're jollyfish," said Neptune.

"Mind your tails, please," said a voice. "Little ones coming through."

The speaker was a large crab, with a trail of tiny crabs scuttling along behind.

"The city's so big," said Emily. "How will we find Slick?"

"I'll take you to where I saw him," said Neptune.

Chapter Five
Glimmer City!

Neptune led them along wide swimways that snaked between buildings. The friends had to concentrate on where they were going, though they would have loved to take a moment to look around. But there was no time to stop!

Neptune turned a corner by a stall

with a sign that said it sold sand-wiches and sponge cakes. Then he stopped so suddenly that Aisha and Emily nearly bumped into him. They ducked beneath an arch and found themselves in a garden.

"This is where Slick was," said Neptune. "Maybe he hid the locket here."

Ripplestripe searched the rockeries, while the girls peered under every flower and frond.

"The locket's not here," said Emily, after a while. "Slick isn't either." She felt very disappointed.

"We're not giving up," said Aisha. "We'll swim through the city looking for him. Let's go." She set off.

"Wait!" called Emily. "Stop! We'll be swimming around for ever if we don't make a plan."

Aisha took no notice, so Emily called again. "*Wait!*"

Aisha glanced back and said, "Speed is important! We must find Slick before he gets away!"

"That's silly," Emily said. "We'll end up chasing our tails. We have to make—"

Aisha spun around. "You don't need a plan to search for someone," she snapped. "You just look!"

The two girls faced each other, nose to nose.

"That's stupid!" cried Emily.

"No, it isn't!" said Aisha.

"Is too!"

"Is not!"

Ripplestripe swam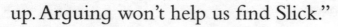
across. "Why are
you bickering?"
she asked.
"Please make
up. Arguing won't help us find Slick."

Aisha and Emily were upset, but neither
of them felt like making up.

Ripplestripe sighed. "If only I had my
lock—"

She broke off as Aisha shrieked in fright.
A long, slinky, brown creature wearing
an old-fashioned diving helmet swooped
around them.

Slick!

He dangled two crystal unicorn keyrings from his paw.

Emily and Aisha's hands flew to their waists. Their plaited seaweed belts were gone!

"You stole our keyrings!" cried Emily

"I love sparkly things!" Slick laughed. Without another word, he swam away.

Aisha put her hands on her hips. "That was your fault, Emily," she cried. "You distracted me by arguing about my plan."

"You haven't *got* a plan," said Emily. "That's your problem. Come on, let's chase him."

Ripplestripe's ears drooped. "Please don't quarrel," she begged. "Please make up and be friends again."

But they were too cross to make up.

"I'm going after Slick," said Aisha. With a flick of her tail, she was gone.

Emily glared. "Well, I'm making a plan!" she yelled.

Ripplestripe raced after Aisha. "Stop!" she called. "Come back! We should do this together!"

But Aisha just kept going.

Slick sped through Glimmer City, turning left and right and disappearing around corners. Aisha had to power through the water to keep up. Then, just as she felt she was going to catch him, something crashed into her.

"Oof!" Aisha was sent tumbling in a whirl of bubbles. She used her arms

and tail to right herself, and there was Ripplestripe, looking alarmed.

"Sorry, Aisha," she said. "I took a shortcut, and suddenly there you were. I couldn't help bumping into you." She looked around. "Where's Slick?"

"He turned left at the Dolly Finn Café," said Aisha, pointing to a building topped with a smiling dolphin cut-out. "He's not far ahead. Come on!"

They rounded the corner in time to see Slick turn into an alley. Aisha and Ripplestripe were there in a couple of seconds.

Slick's way was blocked by a high wall on which was a mural made of pretty coloured shells.

Ripplestripe cried out in delight. "He's cornered!"

Aisha surged forward with outstretched arms and made a grab for Slick. "Got you!" she cried.

He spun around. "You haven't!" he shouted through his helmet. Just as her arms closed around him, he shot upwards, slipping away easily. In a flash he was over the wall, and out of sight.

Chapter Six
A Trick at City Hall

Emily was with Neptune in Seagrass Square. She tried hard to think of a plan to find and catch Slick.

"I think he stole the keyrings because they sparkle," she said. "He likes sparkly things. Neptune," she added, "where is the most sparkly place in Glimmer City?"

Neptune grinned. "Shiny Shell Park. I'll show you!"

They followed a long swimway and dived through a coral arch into the park. Emily thought it was the prettiest place she'd ever seen. Shimmering seaweed grew everywhere, like grass. The coral trees were coloured pale rose pink, creamy yellow, the light blue of a winter sky, even palest lilac. And they sparkled. But the most dazzling things of all were the shells that were arranged into paths around the park. They shone so brightly, it was like they were glowing!

Emily and Neptune followed the paths as they swam around searching for Slick. Emily was about to give up when she

spotted a brown tail disappearing through the coral arch. It was followed by a trail of bubbles from Slick's diving helmet.

"Let's follow his bubble trail," she cried.

But when they reached the arch, the bubbles had disappeared. So had Slick.

Emily buried her face in her hands.

"Are you all right?" Neptune asked.

Emily looked up. "I feel so silly," she said. "If I hadn't wasted time trying to make a plan, we might have caught Slick by now."

She turned away and stopped in surprise when she came face to face with Aisha. "Oh. It's you. Hello," she said.

"Hello," said Aisha.

They didn't smile. They still felt cross

with each other, and hurt by their argument.

Ripplestripe swam between them. "I know it's hard to get on with one another because your hearts are still sore from your argument, but please make up," she begged.

The girls folded their arms. Aisha frowned. Emily saw the cold look on her friend's face, and that made her even more stubborn.

Then Neptune tried. "Even if you won't make up, at least try to work together."

"We have to find Slick," said Ripplestripe. "Not just for the sake of everyone in Enchanted Valley, but for your sakes, too."

Aisha unfolded her arms with a sigh. "Ripplestripe and Neptune are right, Emily," she said. "Finding the Heart locket and our keyrings is more important than being cross with each other."

Emily unfolded her arms, too, although it took an effort. "I suppose so," she said.

"We should work together. Did you see where he went?"

Aisha nodded. "I almost caught him." She looked down. "Then I did something silly."

"I was silly, too," said Emily.

"That's not important," said Neptune. "Speed is."

"And sparkly things!" said Aisha. "That's what Slick loves. Let's use sparkly things to lure him into a trap."

Emily nodded. "That *does* sound like a plan!"

They searched for the shiniest, sparkliest shell they could find. Ripplestripe found a purple one, speckled with flecks of silver and gold. It was as big as a melon, and almost as round. Aisha carried it in both hands as they swam out of the park.

"I don't know which way to go," said Aisha. "Slick's bubble trail has gone."

She heard giggles beside her ear and turned to see a group of jollyfish bobbing beside her. "We know where the bubble-maker is," a blue one chuckled. "We followed it. It was fun popping its bubbles. Pop! Pop! Pop!"

All the jollyfish rolled over and over, gurgling with laughter.

Neptune spoke sternly to them. "Please tell us where he is."

The jollyfish tried to look serious.

"The bubble-maker went into City Hall," said the blue one. He turned to his friends. "Come on, let's tickle lobster tails!"

Neptune took the friends along a wide swimway, towards a shining white castle. "That's City Hall," he said.

"Slick might be looking out of a window," said Ripplestripe. "How can we get to the door without him seeing us?"

Before Neptune could reply, a huge shape loomed above the buildings. It was blue and rubbery and had a giant

stomach. Emily recognised it immediately, thanks to her *Big Book of Nature*.

"A blue whale!" she gasped. "It's enormous!"

Neptune grinned. "I know he's huge, but Zeppo is actually a baby whale," he said.

Zeppo's tail swished slowly. It caused such a swirl that they were all sent tumbling and rolling down the street!

As they righted themselves, Emily said, "Zeppo is the perfect cover! Come on, we can swim under his tummy and Slick will never see us! Then we can confuse Slick by swishing our tails too."

"Great idea, Emily!" said Neptune. "Zeppo, is that OK?" he called up.

The baby whale gave a slow wink.

"That means yes." Neptune beamed.

It was a thrill to creep along with a huge baby whale as he swam slowly above them! Zeppo stopped above the castle entrance, and waved his tail very gently to say goodbye.

Aisha set the big sparkly shell on the castle's front step. Then the four friends hid behind a pillar.

Neptune spoke in a loud voice. "Wow! Whose magnificent shell is this?"

"It's so glittery and shiny!" said Emily.

The doorknob turned and Aisha felt her heartbeat get faster and faster.

"I've never seen anything quite as sparkly!" she cried.

The door opened just a little bit, and

Slick's nose poked out.

"If no one wants it, I'll have it," said
Ripplestripe.

A voice yelled, "No, you won't!" The
door was flung wide and Slick appeared.
"I want it!"

"Now!" Emily cried. "Start swishing!"

They all swished their tails as hard as they could. First they made waves. Then they made swirls. The water churned and bubbled, and Slick tumbled over and over.

"Whoa … whoa … WHOA!" he cried.

"It's working!" cried Aisha. "Keep swishing!"

Slick was soon surrounded by a wall of swirling, whirling, bubbling water.

"We've done it!" cried Ripplestripe. "He's trapped!"

Chapter Seven
Sad Slick

Neptune, Ripplestripe, Aisha and Emily circled around Slick. As the bubbles cleared, his cross face came into view.

"Go away!" he shouted.

"Give us our keyrings," cried Aisha.

"And the locket," added Emily.

"No!" said Slick.

Emily picked up the big shell. "We know you love sparkly things," she said. "You can have this lovely glittery shell if you hand over our keyrings."

Slick laughed. "I didn't take your keyrings just because they sparkle. I know what they're for. You use them to come and go from Enchanted Valley."

Aisha looked at Emily in horror. This was the worst thing ever!

Emily stayed calm and spoke firmly. "Please give them back," she said. "They're no use to you."

"They are," said Slick. "I want to leave the valley, like you do. I don't want to help Selena become queen any more. She spoils everything." His whiskers drooped.

"But I can't stay here. No one will like me, because I *did* help her."

He looked so sad that Aisha felt sorry for him. "If you stop helping Selena, everyone will forgive you," she said. "All you need to do is say sorry – and mean it. Then you can stay in Enchanted Valley and be friends with everyone."

Slick hesitated. "Even Queen Aurora?"

Ripplestripe spoke up. "We know Selena never forgives or forgets, but Queen Aurora is different. She loves us all, and she wants us to be happy and peaceful. That's why she protects us."

Slick frowned, clearly thinking it over.

Emily reached for his paw, but he pulled away. "It's OK," she said. "I won't snatch

the keyrings. I just want to show you that
we *can* be friends. Will you give it a try?"

"We-ell," said Slick. "I will, but I'm
keeping the locket and the keyrings for
now." His little brown face brightened.
"Let's make a deal. If the queen forgives
me, I'll give them back, but if she doesn't
– I'll keep them for ever. Agreed?"

Emily and Aisha shared a worried
glance. It felt risky, but they knew they
could trust in the goodness of Queen
Aurora.

"Agreed," they said together, and Slick
held out a paw for them to shake.

It was just as exciting zooming up in the twisty Corkscrew Current as zooming down! But the higher they got, the more arguments and squabbles they heard. They even saw two striped swordfish fighting a duel! Just above, a little lobster rubbed his eyes, crying. "I squabbled with my sister, and now she won't speak to me," he wailed.

"Things are bad!" Emily called to Aisha. "No one can make up their quarrel while Ripplestripe's without her locket."

"I know," said Aisha. "And I don't like feeling cross with you. Let's hurry!"

They surfaced and swam to the edge of the lagoon, where Slick pulled off his diving helmet. Pearl was waiting to greet them, so they took their mermaid combs out and gave them to her. Once their mermaid tails had gone the friends climbed out of the water and raced to the Friendship Circle.

As they drew near, they saw that even Queen Aurora and the Crystal King were bickering.

The Crystal King was saying, "I know the girls mean well, but they'll never get the Heart locket back."

Aisha and Emily couldn't help exchanging a hurt glance. It made them feel sad that the missing locket was making the king doubt them.

"They *will*!" the queen insisted. "They've never let us down."

The king caught sight of the friends. "There they are! And Slick is with them." He looked pleasantly surprised.

Aurora trotted joyfully towards the group. "I knew you'd make it," she said. "We've come back from the palace to start the festival … if you have the locket, that is?"

Aisha and Emily were pleased to prove themselves. They told their story, and when they got to the bit about forgiving Slick, the queen broke in. "Slick, you have been naughty and mean," she said. "Everyone in Enchanted Valley is at risk because you helped Selena. That's very hard to forgive."

Aisha and Emily held their breath. Surely Aurora would take pity on the little otter. If she didn't, Slick wouldn't return the lockets, the Crystal Festival couldn't go ahead and Selena would demand to be made queen. Worst of all, the girls wouldn't be able to get home.

"But if you are truly sorry …" the queen went on.

Slick looked up at her hopefully. "I *am* sorry, truly."

Queen Aurora smiled. "Then of course I forgive you."

Emily and Aisha breathed sighs of relief as Slick glanced at them. He looked so happy.

"Everyone makes mistakes," Queen Aurora continued. "What's important is that they own up, and try their best to do better."

"Thank you, Queen Aurora," Slick

said. "I really am very, very sorry." The girls truly believed that he meant it!

He had just reached to take the locket from around his neck when there was a crackle of lightning and a violent crash of thunder.

Selena flew towards them out of a dark grey cloud. Sparks shot from her hooves, and her purple eyes blazed with fury.

"Slick!" she screamed. "How *dare* you even think of giving that locket back. Give it to me. Now!"

The otter clutched the keyrings and covered the locket with his paws. He looked terrified, but he bravely held his head high and said, "No!"

Selena reared up. Her eyes flashed. "I'll

show you!" she screamed. Her sparking

hooves sent out lightning bolts.

The girls dived in front of Slick.

"Leave him alone!" Emily yelled.

But Selena raged and stamped her

hooves even more.

Aisha shouted over her screeches, "Can

you see the difference, Slick? Selena is

wild with anger and just wants the Heart

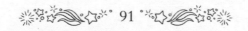

locket for herself. Aurora wants you to give it to Ripplestripe for the whole of Enchanted Valley."

Emily ignored Selena's shrieks too. "Slick!" she cried. "Now is your chance to do the right thing! Give the locket to Ripplestripe!"

Slick clutched the Heart locket. He looked at Selena, who glared at him. He looked at Ripplestripe, whose gentle blue eyes were wide with worry. He looked back at Selena. Her eyes narrowed as she ordered, "Me! Give it to me. Or *else!*"

The girls became worried. If Slick didn't do the right thing, they'd never see their families again.

Chapter Eight
The Crystal Festival

The otter lifted the locket over his head.

Selena threw her head back and laughed. "Good choice, Slick."

Aisha looked at Emily in despair. "Oh no ..."

Emily closed her eyes tight. She didn't want to see Slick give the locket

– and their keyrings – to Selena. But
Aisha clutched her arm. "Look …" she
whispered.

Slick was running to Ripplestripe! As
Selena roared in fury, Ripplestripe dipped
her horn and the otter stretched up to
loop the locket over her head.

Ripplestripe's horn glowed brightly. Emily and Aisha felt gentle warmth fill their hearts. They hugged and said sorry, then hugged again. Everyone else smiled and cuddled their loved ones.

Aurora and the Crystal King gazed into each other's eyes for a moment, then touched their heads together.

Aisha and Emily could feel a sense of calm settle over the valley. The locket was back where it belonged.

Slick padded over to them and slipped their keyrings back into their hands.

"Thank you," the girls said, as they put them back into their pockets.

Selena, meanwhile, flew around, firing lightning bolts into the Friendship Circle.

But when the lightning hit the ground, it melted into a pool of golden water.

The king trotted over to the girls. "Aisha and Emily, I'm sorry for doubting you," he said. "You are the truest friends of Enchanted Valley." He turned to Aurora. "Forgive me. You always choose the right path. You are the most perfect queen."

Aurora lowered her eyelashes. "Thank you," she said softly. "That means so much to me." Aisha and Emily shared a secret glance. The king and queen seemed to like each other very much, and the two friends couldn't be happier.

A cold wind blew as Selena swooped overhead. "Don't look so smug, you lot," she screeched. "I'll have that crown one

day!" She flew away, shrieking, "I will be queen! I *will*!"

Emily and Aisha cupped their hands around their mouths and shouted, "Oh no you won't!"

Aurora turned to Slick. "Thank you for making the right choice," she said.

He looked uncertain. "Am I forgiven?"

"Of course," said the queen.

Aisha and Emily hugged the little otter, his fur like velvet beneath their hands, and his brown eyes shone with joy.

The sun had almost set. It was finally time for the Crystal Festival! Every family in Enchanted Valley had brought their own healing crystals to be charged. Then their magic would keep their owners healthy and happy for another year.

The girls added their keyrings to the pile of crystals in the Friendship Circle. They had to duck as a dragon family swooped in to drop their crystals. Then they waved to Neptune and Pearl, who were floating on the river nearby.

When all the crystals were in place, the king tossed his head. A stream of dazzling light flowed from his horn. It created a glittering path, leading from the edge of the clearing to the Friendship Circle.

The girls were thrilled when their friend Walt Woffly, a guinea hoglet, led

his family out of the trees and along the shining path. Each Woffly carried a bowl of crystals, gathered from the river beside their home. These crystals would be given to the new families in Enchanted Valley.

Finally, the Healing Crystal Unicorns laid their lockets on the glittering pile.

"What happens now?" Aisha wondered.

"We wait for dawn's first light to perform the magic," said the Crystal King. "For now, let's have fun!"

Aurora dipped her horn, sending brilliant sparkles to surround the girls. When they cleared, Aisha and Emily found themselves wearing the most beautiful rainbow-coloured party dresses. The colours shifted and shimmered as they twirled and spun.

"Thank you!" they cried.

Lanterns gleamed in the trees and a great bonfire was lit. Soon the aroma of toasting marshmallows filled the air. Elves and pixies ran around, offering trays of sparkling moonberry fizz and star-shaped strawberry cream tarts.

The Pixie Chicks band played lively music and soon everyone was dancing. Even Slick! It was so much fun that Aisha and Emily barely noticed the time passing, until they realised the stars were starting to fade from the sky. Just before dawn, the dragons – Sparky, Smoky and Coal – set off a stunning firework display. After a dazzling finale, the Crystal King said, "It's time for the ceremony!"

Everyone gathered silently around the Friendship Circle. The lanterns and bonfire flickered out, leaving them in total darkness.

Aisha clutched Emily's hand, and they stood still, holding their breath.

Aurora and the Crystal King hovered

above the huge pile of crystals as the dawn glow appeared over the horizon. The tips of their horns were touching. Around the Friendship Circle stood the four Healing Crystal Unicorns: Rosymane, Firebright, Twinkleshade and Ripplestripe. Aisha and Emily felt a glow of pride to know they had helped save all of their lockets from wicked Selena.

When a ray of dawn's first light struck the royal pair's horns, sparkles shot off in four directions to strike the unicorns' Healing Crystal lockets. The lockets glowed pink, purple, orange and blue. Their magical light spread over the ground inside the circle and into the great pile of crystals.

"Wow!" said Emily, shielding her eyes. "It's almost too bright to look at!"

When the king and queen's horns parted, the glow softly faded.

Aurora turned to the watching creatures. "Our crystals are energised again!"

"Hooray!" everyone cheered, and ran to collect their crystals.

The girls picked up their keyrings. They turned to find the four Healing Crystal Unicorns waiting for them.

"We have a gift for you," said Firebright.

"It's to thank you for your help," said Rosymane.

"And your bravery," added Twinkleshade.

"Hold out your keyrings," said Ripplestripe. She dipped her horn, sending sparkles over their hands. When the sparkles cleared, the girls gasped.

"New crystals!" said Aisha in delight.

Each heart-shaped crystal shimmered first pink, then purple, orange and blue.

"It's like all the Healing crystals in one,"

said Emily. The girls hugged the unicorns, then laid their cheeks against Queen Aurora's velvety face.

"We must go," said Aisha.

"But we'll see you soon," said the queen. "The king and I look forward to that."

He nodded. "We do indeed."

As the girls waved goodbye to their friends, Aurora sent magical sparkles to surround them. They clasped hands as their feet lifted off the ground and Enchanted Valley disappeared from view. When their toes touched down again, the sparkles faded and they found themselves back behind the ice cream van.

"What a fantastic adventure!" said Emily as they ran across the warm sand.

"Let's build our sand palace again."

As they began digging, a shadow fell over them. It was the girl with curly hair.

"Oh no," Aisha murmured. "What's she going to do now?"

The girl moved closer. "I came to say sorry," she said. "It was awful of me to smash your sand palace. I was jealous because it was better than my sandcastle. My name is Chrissy, by the way."

Aisha smiled. "Why don't you stay?" she asked. "We'll build an even better one together."

Chrissy looked surprised, but pleased. "Does that mean you forgive me?"

Emily nodded. "Yes. I'm Emily and this is Aisha," she said with a smile.

"So, we could all be friends?" asked Chrissy.

Emily and Aisha remembered Slick becoming friends with the unicorns, and the way he'd been forgiven.

"Of course!" they said together.

As the three friends began their new sand palace, Emily and Aisha wondered what Chrissy would think if she knew they'd just been swimming with mermaids and riding unicorns across the sky.

But, of course, she never would!

The End

Join Emily and Aisha
for more fun in ...
Heartsong and the
Best Bridesmaids
Read on for a sneak peek!

Emily and Aisha stood in a meadow,
surrounded by clouds of wildflowers.
Petals flew through the air like confetti,
sticking to their clothes and hair.
Aisha reached out to stroke the petals
of a papery red poppy that bobbed
beneath her hand. It was too beautiful
to pick. Instead, she bent to pick a fluffy
dandelion clock and held it up to her best
friend.

"Make a wish and blow!" she cried.

Emily screwed her eyes up tight. "I
wish ... I wish ... I wish we were back

in Enchanted Valley." She took a huge breath and blew, sending the seeds dancing away on the breeze.

Enchanted Valley was a special secret place that the girls had visited on many occasions. It almost felt like a second home to them now!

Read
Heartsong and the Best Bridesmaids
to find out what's in store
for Aisha and Emily!

Also available

Book Thirteen:

Rosymane and the Rescue Crystal

Book Fourteen:

Firebright and the Magic Medicine

Book Fifteen:

Twinkleshade and the Calming Charm

Book Sixteen:

Ripplestripe and the Peace Locket

Unicorn Magic

Look out for the next book!

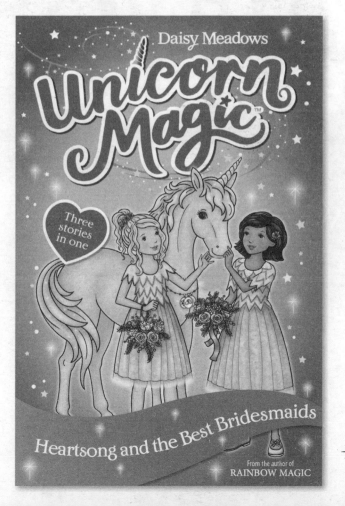

Daisy Meadows

Unicorn Magic™

Three stories in one

Heartsong and the Best Bridesmaids

From the author of
RAINBOW MAGIC

If you like
Unicorn Magic,
you'll love ...

Welcome to Animal Ark!

Animal-mad Amelia is sad
about moving house, until she
discovers Animal Ark, where vets look
after all kinds of animals in need.

Join Amelia and her friend Sam for a
brand-new series of animal adventures!